EASY MATH PUZZLES

For my favorite professional mathematicians,
my brothers Joseph and Nathan.

D.A.A.

2 my husband 4ever,

C.F.

Text copyright © 1997 by David A. Adler
Illustrations copyright © 1997 by Cynthia Fisher
All rights reserved
Printed in the United States of America
First Edition

Library of Congress Cataloging-in-Publication Data
Adler, David A.
Easy math puzzles / by David A. Adler; illustrated by Cynthia
Fisher. — 1st ed.
p.   cm.
Summary: A collection of mathematical riddles involving people,
animals, coins, or food.
ISBN 0-8234-1283-0 (library)
1. Mathematics — Juvenile literature.   [1. Riddles.
2. Mathematics.]   I. Fisher, Cynthia, ill.   II. Title.
PN6371.5A3225   1997   96-30921   CIP   AC
818′.5402 — dc20

EASY MATH PUZZLES

by David A. Adler
illustrated by Cynthia Fisher

Holiday House/New York

People Puzzles

The Crowded Taxicab

A taxicab is on its way to the airport.
1 passenger is in the front seat.
3 passengers are in the back.
How many people are in the taxicab?

Lost in the Rain

2 mothers and 2 daughters
are walking in the rain.
They are all under
the same umbrella.
If there are only 3 women
under the umbrella,
where is the fourth woman?

The Smith Family

Mr. and Mrs. Smith
have 3 daughters.
Each of the 3 daughters
has 1 brother.
How many children
do Mr. and Mrs. Smith have?

Danny and Donna, Brother and Sister

Danny is Donna's brother.
Donna is Danny's sister.
Danny has twice as many sisters
as he has brothers.

Donna has twice as many brothers
as she has sisters.
How many children
are in Danny and Donna's family?

Animal Puzzles

Pets and Legs and Birds and Dogs

Simon has 3 pets.
Altogether, the 3 pets have 8 legs.
Each of the pets
is either a bird or a dog.
How many birds and how many dogs
does Simon have?

More Pets and Legs and Birds and Dogs

Janet has 8 pets.
Altogether, the 8 pets have 26 legs.
Each of her pets
is either a bird or a dog.
How many birds and dogs does Janet have?

Six Legs

Which of these have 6 legs —
a girl, a dog, a bird,
a horse, or a frog?

A Snail's Pace

A snail is in a pool and
it wants to get out.
The side of the pool is 8 feet high.
Each day the snail climbs 6 feet, but
each night it falls back 4 feet.
How many days will it take the snail
to climb out of the pool?

The Dog on the Leash

This dog is on a leash.
The leash is 4 feet long,
but the dog can eat from a bowl
6 feet away.
How is this possible?

Coin Puzzles

Pennies, Pennies, Pennies

Take 3 pennies.
Arrange the pennies
in 2 rows with 2 pennies in each row.

More Pennies

Take 4 pennies.
Arrange the pennies
in 2 rows with 3 pennies in each row.

The Penny Square

How many pennies would you need
to make a square of pennies
with 3 pennies on each side?

Dara's Coins

Dara has 10 coins
that add up to 50¢.
5 of the coins are nickels.
What are the other 5 coins?

Food Puzzles

Soda Cans

These cans of soda cost just 25¢ each.
When you return an empty can
you get 5¢ back.
Jerry has 25 empty soda cans.
How many full cans of soda
can Jerry buy
after he returns each of his empty soda cans?
(Surprise! The answer is *not* 5!)

Eggs for Breakfast

If it takes 3 minutes
to boil 3 eggs for breakfast,
how long would it take
to boil 10 eggs?

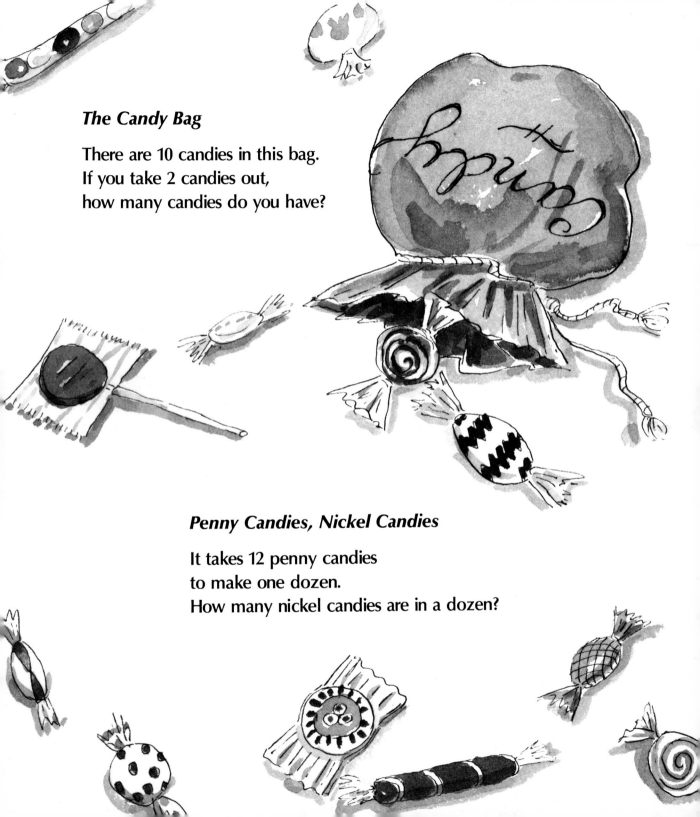

The Candy Bag

There are 10 candies in this bag.
If you take 2 candies out,
how many candies do you have?

Penny Candies, Nickel Candies

It takes 12 penny candies
to make one dozen.
How many nickel candies are in a dozen?

Ears of Corn

Jason goes to the fruit and vegetable store.
There are 14 ears of corn in the bin.
Jason leaves the store with 3 ears.
How much corn remains in the bin?

Sugar, Sugar

You have 2 pots.
One pot holds exactly 5 cups, and
the other pot holds exactly 3 cups.
How can you use only these pots
to measure exactly 2 cups of sugar?

Other Puzzles

How is the Weather?

It's cloudy and cold tonight.
Will it be sunny in 48 hours?

February
1 2 3 4 5
6 7 8 9 10 11 12
13 14 15 16 17 18 19
20 21 22 23 24 25 26
27 28

Calendar Check

How many months
have 28 days?

Seven Eleven

What 2 numbers
can you multiply together
and get 7 as your answer?
What 2 numbers
can you multiply together
and get 11 as your answer?

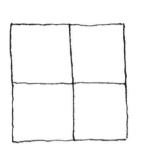

Squares

A square has 4 sides.
Each side is the same length.
Each of the 4 angles is the same, too.

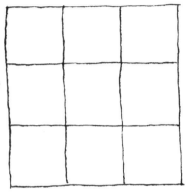

How many squares are in the first picture?
How many squares are in the second?

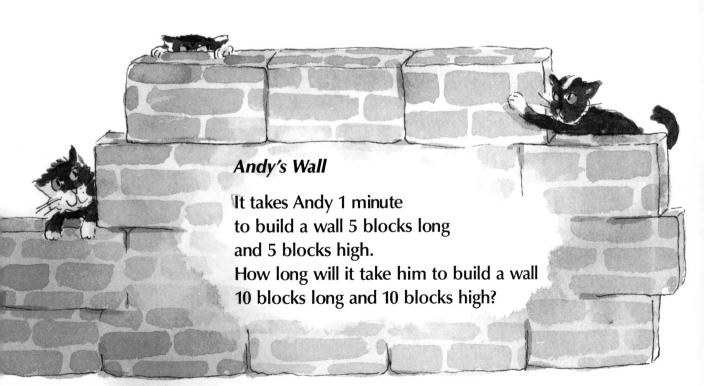

Andy's Wall

It takes Andy 1 minute
to build a wall 5 blocks long
and 5 blocks high.
How long will it take him to build a wall
10 blocks long and 10 blocks high?

Socks in a Box

This box is filled with socks
that are not arranged in pairs.
Some are black and some are white.
If you close your eyes and reach into the box,
how many socks would you need to pull out
to be sure of having a matching pair?

More Socks in a Box

This box is filled with
black, white, red and green socks.
What is the least number of socks
you would have to pull out
to be sure of having a matching pair?

Step Climbing

Paul lives in a 3 story house.
There are 12 steps
between each story.
How many steps would
Paul have to climb
to go from the first story
to the third?

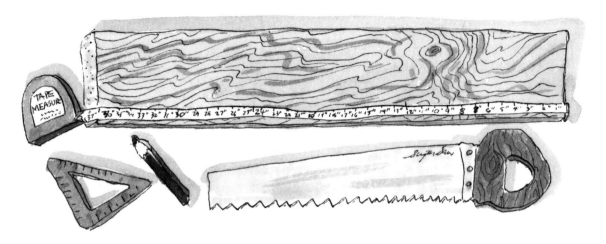

Three Shelves

This board is 3 feet long.
How many times
would you have to cut this board
to make 3 shelves each 1 foot long?

Feathers and Rocks

Which weighs more,
1 pound of feathers
or 1 pound of rocks?

ANSWERS

PEOPLE PUZZLES

The Crowded Taxicab — There are 5 people in the taxi cab, 4 passengers and the driver.

Lost in the Rain — There is no fourth woman. The 3 women under the umbrella are a woman, her daughter and her granddaughter. The woman is a mother. Her daughter is a mother, too. So there are 2 mothers under the umbrella. The granddaughter is a daughter. Her mother is a daughter, too. So there are 2 daughters under the umbrella. There are 2 mothers and 2 daughters under the umbrella, but only 3 women.

The Smith Family — The Smiths have 4 children. They have 3 daughters and 1 son.

Danny and Donna, Brother and Sister — There are 4 children in the family, 2 boys and 2 girls. When Danny counts his brothers, he doesn't count himself, so he has 1 brother and twice as many sisters, 2. When Donna counts her sisters, she doesn't count herself, so she has 1 sister and twice as many brothers, 2.

ANIMAL PUZZLES

Pets and Legs and Birds and Dogs — Simon has one dog (4 legs) and two birds (4 more legs).

More Pets and Legs and Birds and Dogs — Janet has five dogs (20 legs) and three birds (6 legs).

Six Legs — A girl and a dog. (There are other combinations.)

A Snail's Pace — It would take the snail just 2 days to get out of the pool. The first day it would climb 6 feet and fall back 4. It would then be 2 feet from the bottom of the pool. The next day the snail would climb six feet. 2 + 6 = 8. The snail would be out before nightfall.

The Dog on the Leash — No one is holding the leash.

COIN PUZZLES

Pennies, Pennies, Pennies —

More Pennies —

The Penny Square — 8.

Dara's Coins — The other 5 coins are nickels, too.

FOOD PUZZLES

Soda Cans — 6 cans. When Jerry returns the 25 empty soda cans he will get enough money to buy 5 cans of soda. After he drinks those cans and returns the empties, he will get enough money to buy 1 more can of soda.

Eggs for Breakfast — If you put all the eggs in the same pot it would take just 3 minutes to boil 10 eggs.

The Candy Bag — You have 2 candies, the 2 you took.

Penny Candies, Nickel Candies — 12.

Ears of Corn — 13. He left the store with 1 ear of corn and his own 2 ears.

Sugar, Sugar — Fill the 5 cup pot to the very top. Pour that sugar into the 3 cup pot to the very top. Now you have exactly 2 cups of sugar left in the 5 cup pot.

Pizza, Pizza — Slice the pie in half. Slice the pie into quarters. Then pile the quarters one on top of the other and make one more slice, slicing the quarters into eighths.

OTHER PUZZLES

How is the Weather? — No. 48 hours are 2 complete days. In 48 hours it will be nighttime. It's never sunny at night.

Calendar Check — They all do. One month, February, has *only* 28 days.

Seven Eleven — 7 and 1. 11 and 1.

Squares — 5 in the first drawing. 14 in the second drawing.

Andy's Wall — It would take 4 minutes. The 5 by 5 wall uses 25 blocks. The 10 by 10 wall uses 100 blocks. It's 4 times larger than the 5 by 5 wall.

Socks in a Box — The key word is "sure." You could be lucky and pick either 2 black or 2 white socks on your first try. But if you pick 3 socks you are "sure" to have a matching pair.

More Socks in a Box — You would have to pick 5 socks to be sure of getting at least 1 matched pair.

Step Climbing — 24. Paul is only climbing 2 stories, from the first to the second and the second to the third.

Three Shelves — It would take just 2 cuts. With 1 cut you have 2 pieces of wood. With 2 cuts you have 3.

Feathers and Rocks — They weigh the same — 1 pound.